Jeffrey and the Fourth-Grade Ghost

Camp Duck Down

Other
Jeffrey and the Fourth-Grade Ghost
Books

And
Jeffrey and the Third-Grade Ghost

Jeffrey and the Fourth-Grade Ghost

BOOK FIVE

Camp Duck Down

Megan Stine
AND
H. William Stine

FAWCETT COLUMBINE
NEW YORK

This book is dedicated to my nieces and
nephews Hailey, great and small:
Mitch, Jeff, Chris, Ryan,
Jennifer, and Stephanie.
—M.S.

Recommended for grades two to four

A Fawcett Columbine Book
Published by Ballantine Books
Copyright © 1990 by Cloverdale Press, Inc.

Library of Congress Catalog Card Number: 89-91556

ISBN: 0-449-90499-7

Text design by Mary A. Wirth
Illustrations by Marcy Ramsey

Manufactured in the United States of America
First Edition: July 1990
10 9 8 7 6 5 4 3 2 1

Chapter One

Blood dripped down Jeffrey Becker's neck and made a puddle on his white T-shirt. "Mrs. McKane," he said calmly, "I think a tick bit me."

Mrs. McKane took one look at Jeffrey in the rearview mirror of the van and kept on driving.

"Ben said it was a vampire tick," Jeffrey continued, nudging his best friend, Benjamin Hyde. Ben was sitting next to him in the van's backseat.

"Uh, right, Mrs. McKane," Ben said. "I don't think Jeffrey has much time left."

"Ben's an expert on science, you know," Jeffrey insisted.

"That's nice," Mrs. McKane replied. She kept on driving.

"Forget it," Jeffrey said. "I want my money back. This fake blood won't fool anyone."

"Jeffrey," said Mrs. McKane, "the whole fourth-grade class is going camping for four days. Everyone else brought sleeping bags and

1

camping equipment. Why did you bring fake blood?"

"It was free when I bought the plastic poison ivy, the cut-off thumb, and the rubber dead-squirrel family," Jeffrey answered.

"The squirrels are pretty gross, Mom," said Melissa McKane, who was sitting next to her mother. Melissa was Jeffrey's next-door neighbor and one of his good friends.

"I don't want to see the squirrels," Mrs. McKane said firmly.

"Then don't open the glove compartment," Jeffrey warned.

Mrs. McKane rolled her eyes and kept on driving. "You know, Jeffrey, it's been a challenge being your next-door neighbor."

"And it's been a challenge being your friend," Ricky Reyes teased from the middle seat.

"I'll second that," said Ben.

"I'll third that," said Melissa.

"I'll fourth that," said Kenny Thompsen, who was also sitting in the middle seat.

Jeffrey just grinned. Okay, so nobody had fallen for his fake-blood act. That didn't matter. He had a feeling that something strange and fantastic was going to happen at Camp Duck Down. Maybe he'd become pen pals with a wild animal. Or maybe he'd discover a tree no one had seen before—a cross between an apple tree and a walnut tree. The fruit would look delicious, but you'd break your teeth if you tried to bite it. And Jeffrey would take some fruit home to his mom and dad—and maybe by that time his new baby brother or sister would be born. That would be exciting! Jeffrey was hoping that his mom and dad would come to their senses and use the name he had suggested: Hercules.

Just then Kenny Thompsen's voice brought Jeffrey back to reality. "Do you think Max is coming to camp?" Kenny asked. As soon as Kenny said it, everyone shushed him and he clamped his hand over his mouth. But it was too late.

"Max?" asked Mrs. McKane, leaning forward over the steering wheel. "Who's Max?"

Everyone stared at Jeffrey, expecting him to answer—because no one could come up with a convincing story faster than Jeffrey.

"Well, you see, Mrs. McKane—" Jeffrey began.

Melissa's mother laughed. "Jeffrey, every time you say 'you see,' I know a good one is coming right at me."

"But, Mrs. McKane," Jeffrey protested, "I'm

3

not going to make up a story this time. I'm going to tell you the truth."

"You are?" asked Mrs. McKane in disbelief.

"You are?" asked all of Jeffrey's friends in greater disbelief.

"Max is a ghost who was living in my desk in third grade," Jeffrey explained. "Now he's a fourth-grader like us, except he's a little weird. He lived in the 1950s, so he talks the way kids talked in the fifties. He says things like 'coolsville' and 'I dig you the most.' And only the five of us can see him, plus our teacher, Miss Dotson."

Mrs. McKane laughed. "Max is a ghost," she repeated.

"That's right."

"Jeffrey, do me a favor," said Melissa's mother. "Save the crazy ghost stories for the campfire, okay?"

Jeffrey smiled at Ben. "Sometimes, when you don't want people to believe you, you just *have* to tell them the truth," he whispered.

About an hour later Mrs. McKane turned into the parking area of Camp Duck Down. Jeffrey and his friends immediately grabbed their sleeping bags and their packs and jumped out of the van.

"Look! Arrows!" Kenny shouted, pointing to signs with large black arrows.

They followed the arrows out of the parking lot and into a thick woods. Birds in the trees seemed to surround them, chirping noisily. Finally the trees opened into a circular clearing about half the size of a football field. Along the outside of the circle were a dozen small wooden cabins. And in the middle of the circle was a large tree stump, about three feet tall and four feet wide. The stump was covered with painted Indian symbols.

The rest of Miss Dotson's fourth-grade class had already arrived at the camp. They were sit-

ting cross-legged on the ground, waiting for things to start. Jeffrey and his friends quickly joined them.

Then Miss Dotson climbed up on top of the tree stump. She was an older woman, white-haired and small. And she was known for having a very bad memory when it came to names.

"Boys and girls!" Miss Dotson said, turning around on top of the stump and stretching her arms out for silence. "I want to welcome you to Camp Goose Down!"

"Duck Down," Becky Singer said with a sigh.

"Why? Is something going to hit me?" the teacher asked.

"No! It's the name of the camp, Camp Duck Down," Becky answered. Correcting Miss Dotson was one of Becky's favorite activities.

"Oh, yes, of course," Miss Dotson said. "Thank you for reminding me, Betsy. So let's hear it for Camp Duck Down!"

Everyone cheered and whistled as loudly as they could.

Then Miss Dotson introduced the adults who were going to be the cabin counselors. "I'll be in cabin number one and Mrs. McKane will be in cabin number two," she announced, dividing the girls in the class between the two cabins.

Five boys were to go with Jenny Arthur's dad to cabin three. And Arvin Pubbler's father took four boys to cabin four. That left Jeffrey, Kenny, Ben, and Ricky all by themselves.

"Who's going to be our counselor?" Jeffrey asked.

"Well, boys," Miss Dotson said, "at the last minute Robin's father had to cancel. So it looks like you're going to be on your own in cabin number five. Of course, Mr. Arthur will check in on you from time to time. I hope I can trust you."

It took everything Jeffrey had not to jump up and shout, "Totally awesome!" Instead he just took off at top speed, running toward the cabin. Ricky, Ben, and Kenny soon caught up with him, then Ricky took the lead.

A minute later the four friends were checking the place out. It was only a small wooden shack with five folding cots on the floor and two light bulbs hanging from the ceiling. But with no grown-ups watching them, it was going to be perfect.

Happily they unrolled their sleeping bags and began to unpack their gear. But suddenly an extra rolled-up sleeping bag appeared on the fifth cot—the empty cot. Then slowly the bag

7

unrolled all by itself! And as it unrolled, a boy about Jeffrey's age unrolled out of thin air with it. It was Max!

"Hey, Daddy-o's, slip me some skin and let the groove begin," said the fourth-grade ghost. He jumped off the cot and took a comb out of his back pocket to comb his slick black hair. One high curl, which looked a little like a shark fin, dipped over his forehead. Max was wearing his usual outfit: baggy blue jeans with the rolled-up cuffs and a T-shirt with rolled-up sleeves.

"Max, what are you doing here?" Jeffrey asked. "Has my mom had the baby or something?"

"Like, who knows, Daddy-o?" answered the ghost with a shrug. "I made like a banana and split that scene."

"You left home?" Jeffrey said, although it was obvious that was exactly what Max had done. "But you promised me you'd stay at my house so you'd know when the baby came. Only *then* were you supposed to come here to tell me."

"Daddy-o, I couldn't do it. Do you think I'd blow another chance to see *him*?"

"To see who?" asked Kenny.

The ghost's eyes grew bigger as he said the word: "Bigfoot."

"Isn't that just a truck with humongous tires?" asked Ricky.

"Bigfoot, also known as the Abominable Snowman, or Yeti," said Ben, who knew everything a ten-year-old could know about science. "It's a creature thought to live in the upper elevations of the Himalaya Mountains. Lots of people have said they've seen him, but there has never been any scientific proof that he exists— especially not here at Camp Duck Down."

"Daddy-o," said Max, "sometimes you're such a square—I'll bet your plants have square roots!" Then he laughed hysterically for about two minutes at his own joke. "But seriously, I've dug Bigfoot, face to fuzzy face. In fact, the big guy and I have even gone a couple of rounds."

Jeffrey, Ben, Kenny, and Ricky immediately sat down on their cots. "Tell us everything," said Ben.

"Well," Max said very seriously, "for one thing, this happened when things were *really* hip—like, when I was making the third-grade scene for real—not taking the bus from ghostsville. Anyway, my third-grade class came to Camp Duck Down. All the other cats and chicks were bopping around, digging all the camp stuff that's strictly from squaresville—trees, frogs, name tags. But yours truly decided to take a look around the forest because I thought I heard some strange sounds in there."

Jeffrey was starting to get goose bumps listening to Max's story. And he knew he wasn't the only one. Max leaned in closer and looked each one of them in the eyes before he went on.

"Well, Daddy-o's, everywhere I went, I kept digging these weirdo noises. And I got the feeling that something was eyeballing me, something so close I could hear fleas coughing on him. That's when I saw it."

"Bigfoot!" Kenny almost shouted.

Max cleared his throat and shook his head at Kenny. "No, worse. It was a cave. It looked like your everyday spookyville cave, with two trees beside the entrance. But the minute I got inside, I knew there was nothing everyday about this scene."

"Did it have bats?" asked Ben.

"Yeah, but really hip bats, Daddy-o," Max said. "Like, they wore sunglasses. And p.u. city! That cave smelled like the place where old high-top sneakers go to die."

Jeffrey couldn't take it anymore. "Max, was Bigfoot in there?" he asked.

"Like, what do you think was stinking up the

cave the most?" the ghost told him. "But I didn't know he was in there till I tripped over him. They don't call him Bigfoot for nothing."

"What did he look like?" Ricky asked.

"It was darker than darksville, Daddy-o," Max said. "So I didn't see him real well. But he made the word *big* seem puny."

"Was he furry?" Jeffrey asked.

"Did he stand on his back legs or on all fours?" asked Ben.

"Daddy-o's, I didn't ask him to, like, pose for me," said the ghost. "I was too busy trying to find the exit. But then he grabbed me."

"He grabbed you?" Kenny echoed in a shaky voice.

"Yeah. Grabbed me and held me upside-downsville until I was practically coming out of my shoes." Max was talking faster and faster. "And that's just what he wanted. He wanted my shoes—my cooler-than-cool blue suede shoes. So I let the cat have them . . . right between the eyes. Well, Daddy-o's, he dropped me faster than a platter on a jukebox. After that I split the scene immediately, if not sooner. And I didn't stop running until I got back to the painted tree stump where all of the other happy campers were waiting. And I never saw the big guy again."

"Wow!" Ricky exclaimed.

"Major awesome wow," Kenny said. He was breathing hard. "Do you think he's still here?"

"Daddy-o, as long as there are juicy people and cool shoes, that cat is definitely going to hang out." And with that, Max pulled out his comb again and began to comb his hair.

"Sure, Max," Jeffrey said skeptically.

"Jeffrey-o, you wound me the most. You don't believe me?"

"Believe in Bigfoot?" Jeffrey asked. "No way."

Max pointed the end of his comb right at Jeffrey. "Daddy-o, if you doubt me, all I can say is, I dare you to go into Bigfoot's cave! Unless you're too, like, scaredsville."

"Scaredsville? Not me," Jeffrey said, although his voice was trembling when he said it. "Hey, I wasn't scared when I found you, was I? So if I'm not afraid of Big*mouth*, then Big*foot* won't scare me, either."

"Does that mean you accept the dare?" Max asked with a grin.

"Sure," Jeffrey said, still sounding a little worried. "If Bigfoot's out there, I'll find him. I'll find him before we go home."

Chapter Two

Jeffrey, Ben, Ricky, and Kenny stayed up late that night talking about Bigfoot. They talked until everyone was too sleepy to talk anymore. Then they climbed into their sleeping bags and listened silently to the unfamiliar sounds in the woods outside.

Twigs and branches snapped. Was it the wind—or giant footsteps?

Something was out there. Maybe it was just Max, trying to scare them again. Or was it something else, something tall and furry and bloodthirsty, with extra-extra-large feet?

Jeffrey zipped his sleeping bag up tight. In the dark he heard Ricky, Ben, and Kenny doing the same.

The next morning the boys' cabin door opened with a loud bang. Jeffrey bolted up, his eyes half open.

Standing in the doorway was a big hairy creature, big enough to block out most of the morning light. The creature didn't move or say anything. It just stared at the startled boys.

"It's Bigfoot!" Ben shouted as he rolled off his cot and hit the floor with a *thud*.

Ricky woke up when he heard Ben. Ricky, a serious karate student, was the best fighter in the fourth grade. He jumped off his cot, ready to go into a fighting stance. But his sleeping bag was still zipped up, so he fell flat on his face.

Kenny didn't even look. He just scrunched his eyes shut and ducked deeper into his sleeping bag.

Jeffrey still couldn't see who it was. His sleepy eyes wouldn't focus, and his heart was pounding too hard.

"Rise and shine, guys," the creature said.

Oh, no, Jeffrey thought. That's not Bigfoot. It sounds just like Arvin Pubbler's father! Arvin was the most whiny, clumsy, unpopular boy in the fourth grade.

Then the man stepped into the cabin, and Jeffrey saw that it *was* Arvin Pubbler's father—a very tall man with wildly messy hair. He was wearing lime-green sweatpants and a red sweatshirt that was a little tight over his round belly.

His hair stuck out from under his wide-brimmed purple jungle hat.

"Is this the cat who, like, invented color TV, or what?" asked Max, suddenly appearing on the empty cot.

"You want to get up, don't you, fellas?" Mr. Pubbler asked cheerfully. "Don't you? Huh, fellas?"

Oh, brother, Jeffrey thought. He talks just like Arvin. He asks every question three times!

"Now as for you, young man," Mr. Pubbler said, looking straight at Ben, who had finally fumbled around and found his gold wire glasses so that he could see who was talking to him. "My name is not Bigfoot."

"How about basketball belly, Daddy-o?" asked Max.

Jeffrey and his friends laughed.

"I don't see what's so funny," Mr. Pubbler said, since he couldn't hear Max. "My name is Mr. Pubbler and I'm not making jokes, fellas. Now come on. You don't want your breakfast to get cold, do you? Cold breakfast? Is that what you want?"

"What's for breakfast?" Ricky asked.

"Cereal and milk," Mr. Pubbler told them on his way out the door.

The boys dressed quickly and ran outside. Breakfast was being served at the painted stump. There they grabbed small boxes of cereal and cold orange juice. They opened the cereal boxes and poured in lots of fruit and milk.

Jeffrey, Kenny, Ricky, and Ben sat together on a long log. Soon Melissa and her best friend, Becky Singer, came over.

"I hope we choose teams for sports first thing," said Ricky.

"I thought we were going to look for—" Jeffrey interrupted himself to lower his voice. "You know who," he finished mysteriously.

"What are you guys talking about?" asked Melissa.

"Bigfoot," Ben said.

"Bigfoot?" Melissa echoed.

Jeffrey was going to explain to Melissa about Bigfoot, but just then Miss Dotson blew her whistle and called the class together.

"We're going to choose up two teams now for sports and for activities," Miss Dotson announced. "The Red Team and the Blue Team. You'll be on the same team for the next four days, the whole time we're at camp. Whichever team wins the most competitions wins the Camp

18

Duck Down pennant. Now who'd like to be a team captain? How about you, Brian? You can be captain of the Red Team."

"All right!" Brian yelled. "We'll smash the Blue Team! We'll destroy them! All right!"

"Oh, brother," Jeffrey said to Ricky. "Why did she pick him?" Brian was an obnoxious bully and one of the least popular kids in the class.

"And you, Rocky Reyes," Miss Dotson went on. "You can be the captain of the Blue Team."

"Go, Rocky!" Jeffrey teased.

Ricky grinned and punched him in the arm. For the next fifteen minutes Ricky and Brian took turns choosing teams. Ricky picked all of his friends: Jeffrey, Ben, and Kenny. And of course he chose Melissa, since next to him she was the fastest runner and best athlete in the fourth grade. And then he picked four other kids, including Becky Singer. Near the end he even picked Virginia Louise Slimak. She was chosen last because she hated to get dirty. In fact, she hated everything about camp—especially being outdoors.

"That leaves just one extra person," Miss Dotson announced. "The teams won't be even since there are twenty-one in our class. But someone has to have the advantage of an extra person, so . . . Ricky, you can have Arvin Pubbler on your side."

Ricky groaned and Brian laughed.

"Yo, nerds!" Brian called. "Say hello to Arvin—and bye-bye to the pennant!"

"All right, Arvin," Ricky said, trying to be nice to him. "Just do your best and maybe you won't hurt the team too much."

As soon as the teams were set, the class followed Miss Dotson and the other adults down to Jumping Lake. It was a small lake surrounded by tall trees. The canoe races were the first activity, and they were going to be held there.

Two long, heavy plastic canoes sat half on the shore, half in the water. One canoe was blue, one was red. Both canoes were big enough to hold five people.

"Now, for the first race, I need four volunteers from each team, people who already know how to canoe. The second race will be for the students who've never canoed before," explained Miss Dotson.

The Blue Team quickly chose Ricky, Melissa, Jeffrey, and Ben for the first race. The Red Team chose Brian, Jenny Arthur, and two of the strongest, biggest boys. All eight rowers got into their life jackets and headed toward the canoes.

"Not so fast," Miss Dotson called out to them. "Each canoe will have an adult captain: Mr. Arthur for the Red Team and Mr. Pubbler for the Blue Team!"

"Oh, no. We're goners," Ricky moaned.

"But, Miss Dotson," said Mr. Pubbler, "I've never been in a canoe before."

"Don't worry," answered the teacher. "You'll wear a life jacket."

"I don't believe it," Ben whispered to Jeffrey. "He complains worse than Arvin!"

The teams finally got into their canoes. They sat in single file with the grown-ups in the very back. Then they shoved off from the shore.

Miss Dotson started the race by waving a flag and shouting, "Ready! Aim! Fire!"

"Ready! Set! Go!" everyone else called out, correcting her.

And the race was on. Brian's canoe pulled away and quickly took the lead. His team was big and strong.

"Okay, I'll steer," said Mr. Pubbler. "Hey, our boat's broken. Where's the rudder? Okay, nobody panic. You guys just keep your oars in the water."

"Paddles, not oars!" Ben called out as he

pulled his paddle through the water, pushing the canoe forward.

"Stroke, stroke, stroke," Melissa called out, setting a fast rhythm for the four paddlers.

"Not too fast," Mr. Pubbler said, holding on to his hat so that it wouldn't blow off.

"Are you kidding?" asked Ricky. "We're supposed to go fast! This is a race!"

"We're gaining on them," Jeffrey announced.

The rest of the class was cheering and running around the small lake to wait at the finish line on the other side. But Jeffrey was barely aware of them. He kept his mind on his paddle and on the red canoe ahead of them. He and Melissa were paddling on the right side of the canoe. Ricky and Ben were paddling on the left. They all tried hard to stay together and keep a steady rhythm.

The red canoe was about ten feet ahead of the blue canoe. Then Ricky's team caught up a little. Brian saw them coming and tried to paddle faster and faster.

"He's not paddling with his team," Ben said. "And because of the physics involved, all he's going to do is steer his canoe off course."

"Ben, forget science for once and paddle!" Ricky shouted. "We're still gaining!"

Slowly but surely, the Blue Team caught up with Brian's canoe. They were only five feet behind.

"This is too exciting. I've got to get a picture of this," Mr. Pubbler said. He slid the cover off the lens of the small camera around his neck.

"Stroke, stroke," Melissa called out.

They were only three feet away from Brian's canoe. On shore the crowd was going nuts.

"I can't see your faces from back here," Mr. Pubbler said. "I'll get a great shot if I move to the front of the boat."

"Don't move!" Ricky shouted. "Don't stand up!"

"Oh, that rule is just for kids, not grown-ups," Mr. Pubbler said. He stood and started to move to the front of the canoe.

The canoe wiggled under everyone and began to tip. Instantly Mr. Pubbler lost his balance.

Splash! With one loud, wet noise, the race was over for the Blue Team. The canoe, Jeffrey and his friends, the four paddles, and Mr. Pubbler all hit the water at the same time.

"Ha ha!" Brian's laughter could be heard in the distance as his canoe pulled toward shore. The Blue teammates bobbed and floated, thanks

to their life jackets. Then they quickly swam to their canoe. They grabbed on and slowly swam the rest of the way to shore, pulling the canoe by a rope that was attached to it. Ricky was so mad that he wouldn't even look at Mr. Pubbler, who whined and coughed all the way back.

"I knew your team was all wet from the start," Brian said as soon as Ricky and Jeffrey were wrapped up in huge towels.

Ricky threw his towel on the ground. "How'd you like me to push your teeth in so far you'll bite the back of your neck?" he asked Brian.

Jeffrey jumped between the two boys, holding Ricky back. He had never seen his friend get this worked up about winning. "Cool it, Ricky. That's too many words in one sentence. Brian's brain can't comprehend that." He grabbed Ricky's arm and tried to pull him away from the fight. But Ricky wouldn't budge.

"We've got to beat this creep," Ricky said.

"Sure," Jeffrey agreed. "But you know what Max would say if he were here. He'd say, 'Daddy-o, don't get hot. Get cool—and get even.' There's no way we'll lose the next race."

"Right," Ricky said, making a fist and waving it in the air. "Get even! Tomorrow we win for sure!"

Chapter Three

After the canoe races things calmed down at Camp Duck Down. In the afternoon Miss Dotson led the class on a long walk through the woods. There she named every flower and bird they saw—and Ben said she got *all* of the names right! Meanwhile, Jeffrey looked around in the woods and was very relieved to find no sign of Bigfoot's cave.

That night Mrs. McKane made a campfire. Everyone roasted hot dogs and corn on the cob for dinner, and for dessert they made S'mores. Jeffrey and his friends all searched for their own personal roasting sticks, then toasted marshmallows. They put them, bubbling hot, between two graham crackers with two squares of milk chocolate on them.

"Some things never change, Daddy-o," Max said, showing up just in time for the S'mores. "This was my favorite dessert when I was waking and quaking in real lifesville."

Jeffrey laughed and made an extra-large S'more for Max. They sat by the fire, eating the goodies and watching the sun go down.

When it got dark, Miss Dotson took out a ukulele, which looked a lot like a miniature guitar.

"You haven't been feeding that guitar enough, Miss Dotson," Jeffrey said. "It's puny."

Miss Dotson laughed and then sang a song her father used to sing to her, called "My Buddy." Everyone applauded and whistled when she was done.

Then Mr. Pubbler jumped up. He said, "Hey, we know an old song, don't we, Arvin?" He pulled Arvin to his feet, which wasn't easily done because Arvin obviously didn't want to sing in front of everyone. But finally he got up, and he and his father sang "Me and My Shadow." They didn't remember all of the words, and sometimes they didn't seem to be singing the same tune. But everyone clapped and cheered when it was over, which made Arvin and his dad smile as they took their bows.

"Now who would like to tell us a story?" asked Miss Dotson.

"A ghost story!" Robin Dessart said.

"You rang?" said Max, suddenly floating above the fire.

Jeffrey smiled, seeing his friend. Miss Dotson was smiling at Max, too. "That's not what I had in mind," the teacher told the ghost.

"Let Jeffrey tell a story," Becky Singer called out.

"Okay, but I won't tell a ghost story," Jeffrey said, although he knew that wasn't exactly true. "In fact, this is a true story my dad told me before we came to camp." Jeffrey knew that wasn't true at all. For a moment he looked up at the sky, as if he were getting permission from the moon to begin. Around the fire, his classmates grew quieter and quieter until the fire, the wind, and an occasional quick, nervous breath were the only sounds anyone heard. All eyes were on Jeffrey.

"It happened on a night exactly like this— maybe even on this very night—a long time ago. And it happened right here at Camp Duck Down." Jeffrey spoke very softly so that everyone had to be even more quiet to hear him. "Two best friends named Larry and Floyd were camping here for a whole week. They hiked and fished and swam all day. At night they built a big campfire and ate their dinner and listened to the frogs sing on Jumping Lake. Then they went to sleep in their sleeping bags. The first night everything went fine. But on the second night they heard it for the first time."

"What did they hear, Jeffrey?" asked Melissa.

"A voice," Jeffrey answered. "The voice laughed a strange, silly laugh—sort of like Kenny when you make him laugh so hard at lunch his chocolate milk comes out of his nose."

Kenny blushed. "Just tell the story, Jeffrey," he said shyly.

"Well, finally the voice stopped laughing. It said, 'I need to be sweeter.' And then it said it again. Both boys became a little afraid. 'Why'd you say that, Floyd?' asked Larry. 'I didn't say anything. Why'd you say it, Larry?' asked Floyd. They both thought the other was fooling them.

"The next day they went for a long hike in the woods and didn't get back to their camp until dinnertime. They knew right away that something was different about their camp, but they didn't know what it was. Finally Floyd said, 'Some of our food is gone.' And he was right. All the bread, the fruit, the candy bars, the cookies, and the potatoes were gone. All they had left were a few cans of soup and one can of beans.

"That night," Jeffrey said slowly, "the voice came again, but this time it was even louder.

And it sounded like it was coming from the can of beans. 'I need to be sweeter,' the can of beans said. It almost sounded angry. Larry and Floyd couldn't believe a can of beans was talking. So, for about an hour, they looked everywhere for the voice. But they couldn't find it."

"It was an animal in a tree," said Arvin nervously.

"Animals don't talk," Ben told him.

"The next night was windy, and the sky looked like it was going to dump buckets of water any minute," Jeffrey went on. "Larry and Floyd came back to their camp just before the rain started. They built a big fire, but when they opened up their food supply, there was only one can of soup and the can of beans left. Well, both Larry and Floyd hated beans, so they ate the soup and then went to bed hungry."

Jeffrey stopped talking.

"Then what happened?" asked Jenny Arthur.

"Don't tell us!" said Virginia Louise, pulling her long, curly brown hair over her ears.

"Nobody knows what happened," Jeffrey said. "Larry and Floyd didn't come home when they were supposed to. So the police came out to Camp Duck Down to find them. They searched day and night, but they never found a single trace of them. All they found were their two sleeping bags and a gigantic can of beans. It was really late and the search party was really hungry by then. So they opened the can of beans and ate them. And they all said they were the sweetest beans they'd ever tasted."

Some people laughed and some people groaned when Jeffrey finished. Then Virginia Louise said very bravely, "I don't believe a word of it. Beans can't eat people." And with that, she stood and marched to her cabin.

Arvin Pubbler said solemnly, "I'll never eat another bean as long as I live."

They all sang one more song together and then went to their cabins for bed.

Jeffrey was unrolling his sleeping bag when Max appeared, floating on his back above Jeffrey's cot. "Daddy-o, I think I just dug him."

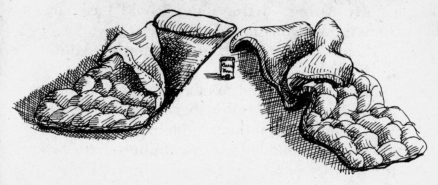

There was no real reason to ask who "him" was, but Kenny did anyway. "Bigfoot?"

"Nobody else," said Max. "It's the perfect night to go looking for him, Jeffrey-o, don't you agree?"

Ghost stories never frightened Jeffrey—at least not when he was the one telling them. But what if the impossible was happening? What if Max was telling the truth about Bigfoot?

"We'll go tonight after everyone's asleep," Jeffrey said.

Suddenly Max said, "Cool it. Parent-o's!"

Right then Mr. Arthur stepped into the cabin. "Just wanted to see if you guys are all right, sleeping by yourselves."

He was kind of a quiet man when he spoke, but he had a big, friendly laugh. Something told Jeffrey that he could trust him.

"Mr. Arthur," Jeffrey said, "could I ask you something? Outside? In private."

He led the way out of the cabin and Mr. Arthur followed.

"I, uh, didn't want to talk about this in front of the other guys," Jeffrey began, "because, uh, well, I didn't want them to be frightened."

Mr. Arthur nodded understandingly. "What is it?"

"Well, these guys think that there's a big creature-thing living here in a cave in the woods," Jeffrey explained. He was trying to keep his voice steady and calm. "You know, Bigfoot. A real people-eater and all that kind of stuff. I tried to tell them, No way. There's no such thing. But they don't believe me. If I could tell them that an *adult* said there's no Bigfoot, then maybe they would believe me."

Mr. Arthur smiled a funny smile and didn't say anything for a minute. He rubbed his gray and black beard. "Jeffrey, I wish I could tell you Bigfoot doesn't exist, but I can't."

Jeffrey tried not to gulp loudly enough to be heard.

"Well, good night, Jeffrey. Sleep tight and don't let the beans bite." Mr. Arthur walked away chuckling.

"Well?" Max asked when Jeffrey came back into the cabin. "Are you going to go looking for Bigfoot tonight?"

"Uh, sure," Jeffrey said hesitantly. "But we have to wait until the coast is clear."

They waited two hours until everyone was asleep. Jeffrey was hoping that his friends would fall asleep, but no luck.

"Okay, get dressed and grab your flashlights,"

Jeffrey whispered.

Ricky, Ben, and Kenny quickly followed Jeffrey's orders. Ten minutes later four flashlight beams led the way out of cabin number five. They walked into the dark night and even darker woods. Of course, now that they were really doing the dangerous part, Max was nowhere to be found.

They started walking slowly away from the cabins, toward the woods that surrounded the clearing. Suddenly they heard heavy, clumping footsteps. Jeffrey's heart pounded and Kenny ran right into Ben, saying, "Bigfoot!"

"Duck down! Hide!" Jeffrey whispered. "He won't see us."

They flattened themselves against the ground and waited. And then a flashlight beam shone on them.

"Hey, you jerks!"

It wasn't Bigfoot. It was even worse—it was Brian Carr.

"Brian, what are you doing out here?" asked Ricky.

"I went to the outhouse," Brian said. "What are you wimps doing?"

"Uh, we're sleepwalking," Jeffrey quickly explained.

"All of you?" Brian asked skeptically.

"Well, we're dreaming about each other," said Jeffrey.

"You guys are doing something and I want to know what," Brian demanded, shining his flashlight right into their eyes.

"It's none of your business what we're looking for," Kenny said. "Oh, boy. Why'd I say that?"

"Don't listen to him," Jeffrey said. "He's talking in his sleep."

"Well, if you won't tell me, I'll bet you'll tell Miss Dotson," Brian said. Jeffrey and Ricky tried to stop Brian, but he squirmed away from them and started calling, "Miss Dotson, Miss Dotson," at the top of his lungs. So Jeffrey and his friends ran back to their cots as fast as they could.

A minute later Miss Dotson arrived at cabin number five.

"I'm very disappointed," she said. "I was counting on you boys to stay here without adult supervision. But I see I should have hired the National Guard instead. What were you doing out there?"

"Stargazing. It was very educational," Jeffrey lied. "What did you say those constellations were called, Ben?"

"Uh, Orion and, uh, Pegasus?" Ben said.

"Right," Jeffrey said quickly. "See, tonight's the exact night when those two constellations meet in the solar plexus and get into a big fight. We just wanted to see the fireworks."

"That's a lame story," Miss Dotson said. "And if you don't stay in your cabin, I'll show you plenty of fireworks. Now get some sleep. You're going to need it. Tomorrow morning is your cabin's turn to clean up after breakfast. But after this little prank, I think you ought to get up extra early and make breakfast for the whole class— all by yourselves! Now, good night."

Chapter Four

"Come and get it!"

At seven o'clock the next morning, Jeffrey was standing at the door of the mess hall, the camp's kitchen and dining room. He banged on the dinner gong with a wooden spoon and yelled at the top of his lungs, "Breakfast *à la* Jeffrey! Come and get it before the bears do!"

Inside the mess hall Ben, Kenny, and Ricky were sleepily setting up breakfast and yawning.

"Guys, you're blowing it," Jeffrey scolded. "You've got to look like you're enjoying this punishment. It drives teachers crazy. Guaranteed." He put on a big smile and shouted again to wake up the rest of the class. "Come and get it while it's hot, hot, hot!"

Jeffrey's cheerful greeting started to work. The rest of the class slowly came out of their cabins and made their way to the mess hall for breakfast.

"What do you want for breakfast?" Jeffrey asked Melissa.

"French toast with strawberry syrup and bacon," Melissa said. She liked to eat food that matched her red hair.

Jeffrey handed her a plate of slightly burned pancakes.

"Jeffrey, is there something wrong with your ears?" Melissa asked with concern. "This isn't French toast and bacon."

"I asked you what you *wanted* for breakfast. I didn't say you'd get it," Jeffrey teased. And he even had time to duck before Melissa's spoon came flying at him.

After everyone had eaten, Miss Dotson announced the day's competition between the Blue and the Red teams. It was a nature scavenger hunt. She gave each team captain a cloth bag and a list of items to find in the woods. The first team to find everything on the list and bring the bag to the painted stump would be the winner for the day.

Jeffrey hurried to finish cleaning up breakfast. As he tied up large plastic bags of trash, he felt a tap on his shoulder. But when he turned around, no one was there—no one Jeffrey could see.

"Like, what's shakin' with the bacon, Daddy-o?" said a voice. Of course it was Max. He soon appeared, holding a blueberry muffin in each hand. "Hey, Daddy-o, this scavenger hunt is perfect-o. While everyone's hot-footing it around the woods, you can go *Bigfooting* it in the big, dark cave. Understand, rubberband?"

Max was daring him again. Jeffrey had to think fast. "Uh, sure, Max. I'd love to look for Bigfoot. But the Blue Team really needs my help with the scavenger hunt. We've got to beat Brian today." He waited to see if the ghost would fall for it.

"Daddy-o, if you were any more chicken, you'd grow drumsticks," Max said as he disappeared.

Okay, so Max hadn't fallen for it. Too bad. Jeffrey wasn't ready to go looking for Bigfoot yet. Although daylight *was* a better time, Jeffrey had to admit.

"Yo, Jeffrey," Ricky called, waving the scavenger-hunt list. "Let's go."

Jeffrey and the rest of the Blue Team ran into the sunlit woods in search of the twenty things on the list. They easily found some of the items on the list. For example, item number 3: Find something that won't burn. So they dropped a small stone into their bag. Item number 11: Find something an animal will eat but a person won't.

"Too bad there's no more of your breakfast left," Melissa joked. "That would be perfect for number eleven."

Instead they caught a fly, and into the bag it went.

"Item number eight," Kenny read aloud. "Find something that is sometimes green and sometimes not."

"Easy," Jeffrey said. He turned to Virginia Louise Slimak. "Get in the bag, Virginia Louise. Every time you see a bug, you turn green."

Virginia Louise, who was wearing her blue windbreaker with the hood pulled tightly around her head, stuck her tongue out at Jeffrey. "How about a leaf?" she said to Ricky.

"Great idea," Ricky said. "Go get one."

"You mean pick it up?" asked Virginia Louise. "With my hands?"

"Never mind," said Becky Singer, dropping a leaf into the bag.

"This is taking too long. We've got to split up," Melissa said. She liked making decisions— for herself and for anyone else who happened to be nearby. "Everybody choose one item, and we'll meet back here in half an hour." She handed the scavenger-hunt bag to Jeffrey so that she could have both hands free.

Pretty soon everyone had chosen something to find. They took off in all directions.

Great, Jeffrey thought as he walked through the woods. He had thirty minutes to look for item number 18. It said: Find what you would be if you were a flower. That was pretty weird, but it was a lot better than looking for what was on Max's list: what Jeffrey would be if he found

Bigfoot! The answer to that one was simple: dead meat!

After a while Kenny came running up to Jeffrey. He had found item number 5, something that proved people had been in the woods. Kenny dropped in a page from an old *TV Guide*. "Great, huh?"

Jeffrey looked at it skeptically. "Maybe the animals have cable."

"Very funny," Kenny said. "I heard the Red Team found twelve things already."

"Well, we've found seventeen," Jeffrey told him.

Melissa soon ran up and added number eighteen, Ben came later with number nineteen, and Ricky number twenty.

"We've got everything! We're going to win!" Ricky said, giving everyone high-fives. "Let's get this bag to the painted stump fast and see what Brian Carr has to say about it."

Just then Ben tugged on Jeffrey's shoulder and turned him around. "Hey, Jeffrey. Isn't that a cave over there?"

Jeffrey looked and then shuddered. It was a cave, all right. A big, dark cave with tall trees on each side of the entrance. Jeffrey's heart sank. It was just as Max had described it. "Uh, no, I don't think that's a cave," Jeffrey said.

"It's Bigfoot's cave for sure," Kenny said.

"Hey, you guys, the game," Ricky reminded them. "We've got to get back to the painted stump before Brian wins the scavenger hunt."

"Totally right," Jeffrey quickly agreed. "Let's go."

"But maybe we won't find this cave again," Kenny said.

"I'll figure out the probability," Ben offered, starting to press buttons on his calculator watch.

"Give me a break," Jeffrey said.

Melissa stepped right in front of Jeffrey and gave him a push toward the cave. "Max dared you to find Bigfoot and you said you would. You've got to do it."

"I can't," Jeffrey protested. "I have to do what the team captain says."

"Okay, go on into the cave!" Ricky snapped. "But make it fast!"

"No problem there," Jeffrey said, turning into the cave. "I'll be back in five nanoseconds."

With a quick salute he stepped into the black cave. The air felt damp and thick, but there was no turning back—not with Melissa blocking the entrance. With every step Jeffrey felt as if he were walking into the open mouth of a hideous

43

monster that never brushed its teeth. The cave smelled awful.

"Arrrggggh!"

What was that? A noise! A faint noise in the distance. It sounded like someone snoring.

Okay, Jeffrey told himself, stay cool. It's just a noise. Noises can't hurt me. Sticks and stones and, of course, my aunt Florence's meatloaf . . .

Slowly he went deeper into the cave. He wished his knees would stop shaking. Why had he fallen for Max's stupid dare? Max? Jeffrey suddenly remembered all of the tricks Max had played on him.

"Max!" Jeffrey called loudly, confident that he knew what was making that noise in the back of the cave. It was just another one of Max's tricks. "Okay, Max, you can stop it. I know it's you trying to scare me."

"Hey, Daddy-o, I'm right here."

Even in the dark Jeffrey could see the faint glow of his ghostly friend standing right next to him. And still the noise moaned and snored in the distance. In fact, it was getting louder.

"But . . . but . . . but . . ." Jeffrey sputtered. His brain was desperately trying to think of a way to explain what was happening. "If you're here, then who's making that noise?"

"I'll give you three guesses and, like, the first two don't count, Daddy-o," Max said. He sounded just as afraid as Jeffrey. "It's Bigfoot, and he's coming this way straight out of bulletsville!"

"Run, Max!" Jeffrey shouted as he took off toward the cave's entrance. "Run for your life!"

"Too latesville for that!" called the ghost as he flew past.

Jeffrey's feet were pounding as fast as his heart. But the monster was behind him. *Right* behind him. It grunted every time one of its big feet hit the ground.

Blam! Jeffrey hit a wall and bounced off it like a pinball. He was dizzy, but he was up instantly and running. Just ahead, a spot of daylight—beautiful, bright, safe daylight. And it was getting bigger and bigger as Jeffrey got closer to it.

"Runnnnnn!" Jeffrey screamed to warn his friends before he was even out of the cave. Just outside the mouth of the cave, Jeffrey's foot slipped on some loose stones. Down he went again, rolling in the dirt. As he got to his feet he saw Max, Ricky, Melissa, Kenny, and Ben racing away from the cave. Jeffrey didn't look back. He took off to catch up with them.

Finally, when he was sure the footsteps had

45

stopped, when he knew he was safe, Jeffrey collapsed against a tree to try to catch his breath. His friends rushed over.

"Did you see it?" asked Ben.

"Too dark. Couldn't find a light switch," Jeffrey gasped.

"Daddy-o's," Max said. "He must have had a hundred feet and twelve big, hairy arms."

"Impossible," said Ben. "Unless it was a whole team."

"I didn't see it," Jeffrey said. He held up two fingers close together. "But it came this close to me—I swear!"

"Hey, Jeffrey," Ricky Reyes said. He was looking around and then suddenly he was looking at Jeffrey angrily. "Where's the bag? Where's the scavenger-hunt bag?"

Jeffrey looked around, too. "I don't know," he said.

"But you were carrying it," Melissa pointed out.

"Where is it?" Ricky asked again, grabbing Jeffrey by the shirt.

"I don't know," Jeffrey said. His head was spinning, trying to remember the last time he had seen the bag. He had forgotten about it when he was running. "I tripped. I tripped when I ran out of the cave. I'll bet I dropped it then."

"Let's go back and get it," Ricky said.

"Cool it, Daddy-o," Max said. "Like, we can't make the scene at Bigfoot's cave. He's not what you'd call friendly."

"I don't care," Ricky said, leading the way back to the cave. "We're going to get the bag and win this game."

They hurried back to the cave and peered at it from behind some trees.

"The bag's gone!" Kenny said.

"Oh, no," Jeffrey moaned. "Maybe I dropped it *inside* the cave."

"Inside? Why'd you take it in the cave with you?" Ricky asked. "That was really dumb."

That was exactly how Jeffrey felt, really dumb.

"Well, I guess we know what this means," Melissa said with a sigh.

"Like, yeah," said Max. "Bigfoot is going to take the bag and grab the prize for the scavenger hunt."

"Maybe," said Ben glumly. "But one thing's for sure. *We lose.*"

When they finally walked sadly back into camp, Brian Carr was already standing at the painted tree stump. The Red Team's scavenger-hunt bag was emptied on the ground, proving that they had collected every item on the list.

But as Jeffrey came closer and began to look at Brian's loot, he noticed something. Lying among the things on the ground were a leaf, a dead fly, a page from an old *TV Guide*, and a bunch of small blue and white flowers.

Kenny noticed it, too. "Hey, *I* found that *TV Guide* page," he said.

"And those flowers," said Jeffrey, "are the forget-me-nots I picked. That's what I'd be if I were a flower."

"And that's the stone I found," said Ben.

"It's all our stuff!" Becky Singer cried.

Anger was turning Melissa's face as red as her hair. "Jeffrey," she said, "after you dropped our bag, Bigfoot didn't pick it up. Big *slime* did! Brian Carr found our bag!"

Ricky kicked the ground as hard as he could. "And he just used it to win the scavenger hunt!"

Chapter Five

"We've been robbed," Jeffrey said, staring in disbelief at all of the things the Blue Team had collected for the scavenger hunt.

But no one was listening to Jeffrey. Everyone on the Red Team was celebrating their victory.

"Brian found all these things by himself," Jenny Arthur was saying to Mr. Pubbler proudly.

"You mean he *stole* them all by himself," Kenny muttered.

Ricky walked away from his friends toward a clump of trees far away from everyone.

"He's mad," Melissa said, feeling bad for Ricky.

Jeffrey nodded. He felt awful and he wanted Ricky to know he was sorry. He walked over to the trees. "Ricky—" he started to say, but his friend interrupted him.

"Don't tell me any of your stupid stories, Jeffrey," Ricky said harshly. "They aren't funny."

"I wasn't. I was going to say I'm sorry. I'm sorry I dropped the bag."

"I mean, you went running off with a ghost chasing more ghosts and you blew everything. We could have won the game easy and wiped that stupid smile off Brian Carr's face!" Ricky picked up some branches and propped them between two large rocks. Then he quickly chopped them in half with a strong karate chop. "Why'd I ever become friends with you, anyway?"

"Because I wouldn't call you a jerk even when you say something stupid like that," Jeffrey said in a quiet voice. "And because I'm not a quitter. We can still win the camp pennant if we win tomorrow's games. And because while you've been chopping kindling for the fire with your bare hands, *I* have been creating a guaranteed, solid-gold, no-fail plan for getting back at Brian Carr once and for all." Jeffrey waited. He knew there was no way Ricky Reyes could resist hearing the details of his revenge plan. And he was right.

"Okay," Ricky said. He stopped breaking branches. "What is it?"

"*Pssst.* Jeffrey! Ricky!" It was Melissa. "Come here," she whispered. She held a finger

51

to her lips, warning them to come quietly. Jeffrey looked at Ricky and shrugged. His revenge plan would have to wait.

Silently the two boys crept over to where Melissa was hiding. She was crouched in some bushes under the window of cabin number two. She motioned them to get down, pointed to the window, and said, "Listen."

Inside the cabin Jeffrey could hear Mr. Arthur's voice. He was laughing, and a woman was laughing, too. It was Melissa's mother.

"I just couldn't resist," Mr. Arthur was saying. "Jeffrey asked me last night if there was such a thing as Bigfoot. So, of course I let him think the answer was yes. I mean, after all the stories he's told us . . ."

"I know," agreed Mrs. McKane. "It would have been hard to resist."

"So," Mr. Arthur went on with a chuckle, "when I saw him near this old deserted cave where Bigfoot is supposed to live, I slipped in first and waited for him. I made some strange, growling sounds just for starters. *Ooooaaargh!* And when he got close enough, I started chasing him."

Mrs. McKane was laughing. "I can just see his face," she said. "It sounds like you did the impossible—you beat Jeffrey Becker at his own game!"

"And it was worth it," Mr. Arthur told her. "Besides, I gave him a thrill he'll remember all his life. Sometimes I wish I were a kid again."

Jeffrey and his friends stayed hidden a minute longer until Mr. Arthur and Mrs. McKane left the cabin. Then they crawled from the bushes, slinking away like cats in the rain.

"Jeffrey, you were suckered," Melissa said when they were safely away. "And by a grown-up!"

"This is the worst day of my life," Ricky said.

"First we lose the scavenger hunt, and now we find out there's no Bigfoot! It was all a complete waste!"

"Yeah. And what's the matter with Mr. Arthur?" Melissa asked indignantly. "Doesn't he know he made Jeffrey look like a complete jerk?"

"There's nothing new about that," Ricky said with a smile.

"Hey, look, Jeffrey is tying his shoelace. That means he's getting an idea," Melissa said.

"Yeah, but it's a double knot," Ricky pointed out. "What does that mean?"

"It means I don't want my shoe to come untied," Jeffrey said, standing up with a calm look on his face.

"So what's your idea?" Ricky asked.

"It's the revenge plan I was going to tell you about," Jeffrey said. "Only instead of just getting Brian Carr, now I'm going to get Mr. Arthur, too."

"How?" Ricky asked. "And it better be good."

"Tonight Mr. Arthur and Brian Carr are going to enter a strange, unearthly world without time or space," Jeffrey said in a mysterious voice. "Tonight they're going to enter . . . The Jeffrey Zone."

■   ■   ■

At midnight Jeffrey sneaked into cabin number three, where Brian Carr and Mr. Arthur were sleeping. Jeffrey went straight to Brian's cot and tried to wake him by poking him in the side.

"No fair," Brian muttered as he rolled over to get away from the poking.

I've got his attention, Jeffrey thought. Now to start the confusion. "Mr. Arthur, wake up," Jeffrey whispered. "Wake up."

Brian sat up and burped loudly in Jeffrey's face. "What do you want, turkey face?"

Jeffrey pretended to be surprised to see Brian. "Oh, it's you, Brian. I thought you were Mr. Arthur," he said. "Go back to sleep. You don't want to hear anything about this." Jeffrey moved over to Mr. Arthur's cot.

"Hear about what?" Brian asked, waking up.

It's working, Jeffrey thought. He wants to know what's going on. But Jeffrey ignored Brian's question and tapped Mr. Arthur on the head. "Mr. Arthur, Mr. Arthur."

"Huh? What? Jeffrey? What is it?"

"It's Kenny," Jeffrey told him. "Kenny went to the mess hall to sneak a late-night snack. But he never came back and now I'm scared."

"Maybe he's just having a long snack," Mr. Arthur said. "How long has he been gone?"

"Two hours," Jeffrey said, turning up the panic in his voice.

"Two hours?" Mr. Arthur threw his covers off and jumped to his feet. "We'd better check it out."

"Okay," Jeffrey said. "Brian, you'd better stay here."

Of course, telling Brian *not* to do something was a guarantee that he'd disobey.

"I'm coming," Brian announced, grabbing his flashlight.

The three of them hurried along the path from the cabin to the mess hall. My plan is working, Jeffrey thought, smiling in the dark. So far, so good.

"Look! There are no lights on inside," Jeffrey said, pointing to the mess hall.

The front screen door squeaked when they opened it, and the wood floor creaked as they stepped in.

"Kenny!" Mr. Arthur called.

"Yo, Kenny!" Jeffrey yelled.

"Hey, geek snot!" shouted Brian.

No one answered.

"Maybe you'd better look in the kitchen," Jeffrey said in a nervous voice. He followed as Mr. Arthur led the way. At the kitchen door Mr. Arthur tried to snap on the light switch, but nothing happened. Jeffrey had unscrewed the light bulb.

"Oh, no!" Jeffrey shouted, shining his flashlight at the middle of the kitchen floor. "It's Kenny's shoes," he said, pointing dramatically, "but no Kenny."

"Wait a minute. What's going on?" Mr. Arthur asked, sounding suspicious.

Suddenly a deep voice came from somewhere in the dark. "I need to be sweeter," said the voice.

"Is that you, Kenny?" Mr. Arthur asked, shining his light all around the room. "Come on out. The joke's over."

But the voice spoke again. "I need to be sweeter," it said.

Mr. Arthur shone his light on Jeffrey. "Did you say that, Jeffrey?" he asked.

Jeffrey shook his head solemnly and tried not to laugh. He could see Max sitting cross-legged about five feet off the ground, right in front of Brian. But he knew that Brian and Mr. Arthur couldn't see Max.

57

"All right, guys. What's going on?" Mr. Arthur was beginning to sound angry.

"Didn't you dig me? I said, I need to be sweeter!" Max yelled.

"Oh, no! It's coming true!" Brian took a deep breath and then stiffened. "It's that story Jeffrey told around the campfire," he gasped. "The can of beans that ate Larry and Floyd!"

"You mean Kenny was eaten by a can of beans?" Jeffrey exclaimed.

"Jeffrey, get serious," said Mr. Arthur. "Cans of beans don't talk."

Suddenly a pantry door opened all by itself—thanks to Max. And in their flashlight beams Mr. Arthur and Brian saw a giant-sized can of beans sitting on the pantry shelf. It had a small red cape draped around it. The cape was really a red T-shirt, but Jeffrey had tied it on to look like a cape.

"Who says beans don't talk?" Max asked spookily. "Like, maybe we don't talk because nobody is hip enough to lay the right questions on us."

"That must be a really old can of beans," Mr. Arthur said. "Nobody's talked like that since the fifties."

Max flew around the room opening one cupboard door after another. Soon every cupboard in the kitchen was open. The shelves were filled with boxes and bags and cans of food, all lined up like an army.

"What's happening?" Brian yelled in a panic.

He ran for the kitchen door, pulling and rattling the doorknob with all his strength. "We can't get out of here!" he screamed in the dark. "The door's locked!"

"You stir us and fry us and bake us and broil us, and then you eat our hearts out," Max said, wiggling the giant can of beans as if it were talking. "Well, now it's *our* turn!"

"What does he mean?" Brian whined. "What's he going to do?"

"Daddy-o, I mean, I'm just like everyone else. I need to eat three square meals a day. And you cats are the squarest meals I've seen in a long time!"

Jeffrey backed out of the way and hid in a corner where he could laugh as hard as he could without being heard.

"This can't be happening," said Mr. Arthur, trying to duck the flying can of beans. "I'm going to wake up any minute now."

Brian was running around the kitchen in panicked circles, shouting, "No fair. You can't eat me! I'm only nine years old."

"No sweat, Daddy-o. You qualify as a kid's meal!" Max said. "Prepare for a bean bomb, you bean bags!"

Max flew high into a corner of the room and quickly opened the can of beans. Of course, to Mr. Arthur and Brian, it looked like the can was opening itself. Then the giant can flew up into the air, tipped, and *swoooooshsplat!* All of the juicy, soft baked beans plopped right on their heads.

"I'm being eaten alive!" Brian shouted as if those would be his last words on earth.

While Brian and Mr. Arthur were busy wiping off the slippery beans, Max and Jeffrey sneaked

out of the mess hall. They ran back to cabin number five.

"How'd it go?" Ben asked anxiously.

"What happened?" asked Ricky.

"Mission accomplished," Jeffrey announced. He filled them in on every detail, and his friends quietly cheered.

"Hey, everyone's waking up out there," Kenny reported from his watch post at the cabin window. "I see Mr. Pubbler stumbling toward the mess hall."

"Too bad we won't be there to hear Brian's and Mr. Arthur's explanations for what happened," Jeffrey said.

"Daddy-o, you know what everyone's going to say," said Max with a grin. "They're going to tell those two cats they're full of beans!"

Everyone laughed at Max's joke. It felt like it had been years since the five friends had had something to laugh about.

"Hey, you guys, I say we get some sleep," said Jeffrey. "And then tomorrow we beat the pants off the Red Team."

Everyone agreed.

"Yeah," Ricky said. His eyes were intense, and his hands were clenched into fists. "Tomorrow—it's win or die!"

Chapter Six

The next morning Jeffrey awoke feeling a mix-
ture of things. He sort of felt good because of
the great bean trick he and Max had played on
Mr. Arthur and Brian last night. But he sort of
felt disappointed, too. So far, nothing really
spectacular had happened at camp. There was
no Bigfoot—that had just been one of Max's fa-
mous pranks. And his team was losing the camp
competition, too. What had happened to that
feeling Jeffrey had had on the way to camp, the
feeling that something strange and fantastic was
going to happen? Maybe it would happen today.
There was still one day left, and to Jeffrey it
didn't sound very promising.

While Jeffrey was eating breakfast at a picnic
table under some trees, Mr. Arthur came looking
for him. He sat down beside Jeffrey and kept
his voice low so that only Jeffrey could hear him.

"Jeffrey, I don't know what happened last

night, but I'm telling everyone Brian and I got into a silly mood and we got into a food fight," he said. "Got that? A food fight. And I expect you to back me up."

"Not real believable, Mr. Arthur," said Jeffrey.

Mr. Arthur frowned. "Jeffrey, it was too dark for me to see exactly how you made the can of beans fly and talk, but I know there had to be a trick to it. How did you do it?"

"I didn't do anything," Jeffrey said with a smile. And he *was* telling the truth. "You know what I think, Mr. Arthur? I think you had a close encounter with *Bigfoot*."

"There is no Bigfoot," Mr. Arthur said.

"But, Mr. Arthur, you told me there was!" Jeffrey protested, pretending to be hurt and totally surprised.

"So that's it." Mr. Arthur cleared his throat uncomfortably and stood to leave. "Okay, we're even. Let's both drop it."

"It's a deal," Jeffrey said with a small smile.

After breakfast Ricky made the entire Blue Team line up by the painted stump for a pep talk before the games began.

"Guys, I just have one thing to say, just one word," Ricky said. "*Win*. It's the most important

63

word there is." He stared at each person on the team. Jeffrey, Ben, Melissa, Becky, Virginia Louise, Kenny, Chris McClure, Andrew Goodwin, Marlie Marx, and finally Arvin Pubbler. "If you don't think you can win, don't even try. Got that?"

Then Ricky went off by himself to do some karate exercises and get focused.

After Ricky left, Mrs. McKane came over and wished everyone good luck. Then she offered an extra T-shirt to Virginia Louise, so she wouldn't have to worry about getting her own T-shirt dirty. Jeffrey decided that even though she'd thought Mr. Arthur's hoax was funny, Mrs. McKane was all right.

A few minutes later Miss Dotson blew a whistle. That meant it was time for everyone to go to the large open field that lay at one end of the camp. All over the grassy field there were starting lines and finishing lines for the different events. The starting lines were marked on the ground with yellow spray paint. The finishing lines were marked with long green streamers tied between two trees.

Miss Dotson explained that this was the last day of competition. There would be running races, jumping races, throwing competitions, and more—eight different events in all. If the Blue Team won all eight events, they could sweep the camp competition and win the pennant.

The first race was a forty-yard hurdles dash, with a special twist to it. In this race the hurdles turned out to be wide mud puddles.

"It's a snap," Melissa said, coiling and tucking her long ponytail under her lucky Red Sox cap. She was running for the Blue Team against Brian Carr on the Red Team.

Miss Dotson blew her whistle and the two runners took off. When they came to the first puddle, Melissa cleared it easily. But Brian Carr seemed to leap into the air and dive straight into the mud. And then, even stranger, he stayed in the mud. It looked like he was splashing around on purpose—and swimming.

A minute later Melissa crossed the finish line, first and fastest.

"No fair!" Brian shouted. "Someone pushed me into the mud puddle. I couldn't get out."

As soon as Jeffrey heard that, he knew that Max was there. He must have pushed Brian into the puddle and then held him there. But Max was staying completely invisible. Even Jeffrey couldn't see him.

"Brian," said Miss Dotson, "it looked to me like you were having so much fun, you didn't *want* to get out of the puddle. So Melissa's the winner for the Blue Team. The sack race is next."

Brian grumbled, but Miss Dotson ignored him, and the next racers lined up. For this race Arvin Pubbler, Ben, and Marlie Marx lined up against three of the Red Team members. They had to hop to the finish line with their legs inside burlap sacks.

Tweeeeeeeet! The whistle blew and a moment later the racers were off as fast as they could go. All except Arvin. He was taking it nice and slow, hopping very small hops so that he wouldn't fall down. But before anyone knew what was happening, the three Red racers had fallen down and Arvin was standing at the finish line.

"No fair!" Brian shouted, running to Miss Dotson after the race was over. "Somebody put soggy oatmeal in my team's bags."

"Well, Byron," Miss Dotson said to Brian, "it looked to me like Arvin practically *flew* to the finish line. I guess it's a case of the tortoise beating the hare again. The Blue Team wins that one."

Ricky got a funny look on his face when he heard that, and he pulled Jeffrey aside. "We've got to find Max," he said. "I think he's here trying to help us win."

"I know, but he's staying invisible. Even I can't see him," Jeffrey said.

"Hey, Daddy-o's, let the games begin," said the ghost, making a sudden appearance.

"Max, did you make Arvin fly? And did you put oatmeal in their sacks?" Jeffrey asked.

"Daddy-o, I cannot tell a lie . . . because the truth is a lot funnier. I even cooked it myself, with cinnamon and brown sugar just the way I dig it the most. Now I'm trying to line up an alligator for the leapfrog race."

"No more tricks, Max," Ricky said angrily. "I mean it. I want to beat the Red Team fair and square."

The ghost frowned. "If you play fair, it'll definitely be square, Daddy-o," he said. But then he shrugged and floated up into a tree. He sat there watching the rest of the races.

During the next two hours, the Blue Team won five out of five races. Ricky easily won the tree-climbing contest. And in the throwing contest Melissa threw the ball so far into the woods that no one could find it, so she had to be declared the winner. And Becky and Kenny won the three-legged race.

Finally, in the middle of the afternoon, it was time for the last event of the camp competition. It was a relay race around the camp grounds. Andrew Goodwin would run the first leg, from the painted stump to the outhouse. Ricky would run from the outhouse to the lake. As soon as he got to the lake, Virginia Louise Slimak would start running to where Jeffrey was standing, at the wishing well. Then Jeffrey would run a hundred yards to the finish line, back at the painted stump.

Once again Miss Dotson blew her whistle to start the racers, and the crowd cheered their teams on. Andrew Goodwin got off to a strong lead. He left all the other runners far behind him. When he finished his part of the relay race, Ricky took off.

From his spot near the wishing well, Jeffrey couldn't see the whole race. So he craned his neck, trying to see Ricky somewhere near the lake. But instead of Ricky, Jeffrey suddenly saw another familiar face. It was his father! Mr. Becker was walking across the clearing from the back of the crowd to the front.

"What are you doing here?" Jeffrey shouted.

But before his father could answer him, another voice pierced the air.

"Run, Jeffrey!"

Jeffrey's head snapped toward the sound. Virginia Louise was practically going to run him down. She was coming straight at him, holding out the baton, a blue-painted stick.

"Take it!" she shouted.

Jeffrey grabbed the stick and took off running, but he couldn't help looking to the side to try to find his father again. What *was* he doing at the camp? Was Jeffrey in major trouble again? Did it have something to do with dumping beans on Mr. Arthur?

While Jeffrey was looking for his dad, the Red Team's runner was sneaking up beside him— and taking the lead!

And then, all of a sudden, Jeffrey realized why his father had driven for four hours into the hills where Camp Duck Down was. It was the baby! His mom must have had the baby! Something strange and fantastic had happened after all!

Jeffrey poured it on, running faster than he had ever run in his life—even faster than when Bigfoot was chasing him! He *had* to get to the finish line fast so he could talk to his dad and hear all about the baby.

Everyone was cheering for Jeffrey, who kept running at top speed until he crossed the finish line. The Blue Team went wild and surrounded him.

"First place!" Ricky yelled, pounding Jeffrey on the back.

"You were first," Kenny said, jumping up and down.

"Win, place, and the whole show, Daddy-o!" Max said.

"Thanks," Jeffrey said, smiling. Then he turned to look for his father. "Have you guys seen my dad?" he asked. But nobody heard him. They were all talking and cheering at once.

Ricky pushed the whole Blue Team back to the painted stump. "Come on. Miss Dotson's waiting to give out the awards."

Just as she had done the day they arrived, Miss Dotson stepped up onto the stump and stretched out her arms for silence. "Our days at Camp Duck Down are almost over," she said. "I'm sure we all feel that we've learned a lot about living and working together. And when we work together as a team there are no losers— only winners. Now, will the team captains please come up." She pulled out a large blue pennant with the words CHAMPION CAMPERS written in silver glitter and handed it to Ricky for the Blue Team. Then she gave Brian a large red pennant with ALL-STAR CAMPERS written in silver glitter.

"But who won the competition?" asked Ricky.

"I told you. We're all winners," Miss Dotson said.

"Yeah, but the Red Team was the main winner," Brian said. "We're the All-Stars."

"Oh, yeah?" argued Ricky. "And what do you think the Blue Team is?"

"A bunch of baked potatoes," Brian said.

"Keep dreaming, Brian," Ricky said. "Our pennant says champions."

Who cares? Jeffrey thought. It's just a race. But I have a new little brother or sister! As he was looking around for his father, he suddenly felt a hand closing on his shoulder.

"Dad!" Jeffrey said, turning around. "I was looking for you. It's the baby, isn't it?"

Mr. Becker nodded and pulled Jeffrey away from the crowd.

"Wow!" Jeffrey exclaimed, jumping up and down. "Did you name him Hercules?"

"Let's start at the beginning," said Mr. Becker. "It's not a boy."

"It's a girl?" Jeffrey asked, blinking with surprise.

"Is there another choice?" Mr. Becker said, laughing and giving Jeffrey a hug. "Yes, it's a girl and we've decided to name her Lindsay."

Jeffrey tried out the name in his mind: Lindsay Becker.

His father smiled. "Do you want to come home early and see her?"

Jeffrey tried to speak, but he was too surprised or excited or something. So he just nodded and said, "Will she know who I am?"

"Not at first, but very soon," his father promised.

"I gotta pack up," Jeffrey said. He raced toward his cabin, not stopping to say anything to anyone. But Melissa, who always knew a hot scoop when she saw one, followed him into the cabin.

"I'm a brother!" Jeffrey shouted, smiling his head off. "I have a sister! I'm going home to meet her right now. Tell everyone!"

"Can I come over the minute I get home?" Melissa asked.

"Sure. But remember: *I'm* going to teach her how to play baseball."

"We'll argue about that later, Jeffrey Becker,"

Melissa said with her hands on her hips.

Then Jeffrey ran with his pack and his sleeping bag to the parking lot where his father was waiting. But as they started to pull out of the parking lot, Ricky came running up to the car.

"Jeffrey!" Ricky called, waving the big blue pennant. "We want you to take this. It's sort of like a baby gift to your new sister from us."

"Thanks, Ricky," Jeffrey said, beaming at his friend.

"Well, here she is." Mr. Becker started the car and handed Jeffrey some instant photos of the new baby. "You know, with the baby, things are going to be a little strange around the house— not that they haven't been strange enough with you, Jeffrey. Anyway, I think she's really lucky to have you for a brother."

"Thanks, Dad," Jeffrey said, staring at the fat pink baby in the photos.

"And, like, that's only half the story," said a voice from the backseat. Jeffrey's head whipped around.

"Max?"

"No, I told you, we named her Lindsay," Mr. Becker said.

Jeffrey stared at Max in the backseat and gave him a silent what-are-you-doing-here? look.

"Relax, Daddy-o. Your little sister is going to get two brothers for the price of one! Babies are a total gas—and I don't mean from burpsville. In fact, yours truly can't wait to check this chick out. Diaper city, here I come!"

Here's a peek at Jeffrey's next adventure with Max, the Fourth Grade-Ghost:
BIG BROTHER BLUES

Max the ghost laughed as he floated over to Jeffrey's baby sister. "Hey, dig this, Daddy-o," he said, making himself invisible. He placed the baby's hands on the crib's bars and started to make her stand up.

"Jeffrey, do you see that?" Mrs. Becker cried. "Lindsay is trying to stand! She's only two and a half months old, and she's trying to stand! She's a genius! Make sure she doesn't move. I'm getting the camcorder!" She rushed out of the room.

As soon as she was gone, Max gently laid the baby down in her crib.

"Thanks a lot, Max," Jeffrey said. "Now my mom will talk about Lindsay and nothing but Lindsay *all day*. Why don't you ever help me get some of the attention around here?"

"Sure, Daddy-o, no sweat. Like, what did you have in mind?"

"What *do* I have in mind?" Jeffrey asked himself out loud. "How about when my mother comes back, I'll tell her I can do something really cool and then you make it happen."

ABOUT THE AUTHORS

Bill and Megan Stine have written many books and stories for young readers including several in these series: *The Three Investigators*; *Wizards, Warriors, and You*; and *Find Your Fate: Indiana Jones*. They live in Atlanta, Georgia, with their son, Cody.